BY **Andrea Zimmerman** AND **David Clemesha** • PICTURES BY **Karen Barbour**

Greenwillow Books, *An Imprint of* HarperCollins*Publishers*

 Manufactured in China.
www.harperchildrens.com Gouache paints were used to prepare the full-color art.
The text type is 18-point Triplex Extra Bold.

Library of Congress Cataloging-in-Publication Data. Zimmerman, Andrea Griffing.
Fire! Fire! Hurry! Hurry! / by Andrea Zimmerman and David Clemesha ; pictures by Karen Barbour.
p. cm. "Greenwillow Books." Summary: Captain Kelly and his fire fighters must
delay their delicious dinner because they keep being called to put out fires.
ISBN 0-06-029759-X (trade). ISBN 0-06-029760-3 (lib. bdg.)
[1. Fire fighters—Fiction. 2. Animals—Fiction.]
I. Clemesha, David. II. Barbour, Karen, ill.
III. Title. PZ7.Z618 Fi 2003 [E]—dc21 2002067858
1 2 3 4 5 6 7 8 9 10 First Edition

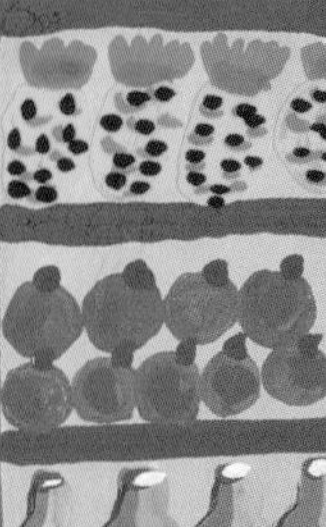

GREENWILLOW BOOKS

To all the good firefighters who give little children tours of the fire station
—A.Z. and D.C.

For the firefighters
—K.B.

KELLY

Captain Kelly loves being a firefighter. He and the other firefighters stay at the station all night, waiting to put out fires.

Tonight Captain Kelly has made a
delicious spaghetti dinner for his friends.
The firefighters sit down and start to eat.
But suddenly—

DING! DING! DING! DING! The alarm rings.
They run to the fire truck.

WOOOOOOO!
Captain Kelly drives quickly.
Where's the fire?
"Help! Help!"

Flowers

There—at the flower shop!
Captain Kelly hooks up the hose to the hydrant.
Fire! Fire! Hotter! Hotter!
Hurry! Hurry! Water! Water!
The team works hard together.
Can they put out the fire?

Yes!
The flower shop owner gives the firefighters a present—
a beautiful bouquet of flowers.
"Bye-bye." The firefighters wave.
Captain Kelly drives them back to the station.

Now Captain Kelly and the other hungry firefighters sit down to eat their delicious spaghetti dinner. But suddenly—

DING! DING! DING! DING! The alarm rings.
They run to the fire truck.
WOOOOOOO!
Captain Kelly drives quickly.
Where's the fire?
"Help! Help!"

There—at the toy shop!
Captain Kelly hooks up the hose to the hydrant.
Fire! Fire! Hotter! Hotter!
Hurry! Hurry! Water! Water!
The team works hard together.
Can they put out the fire?

Yes!
The toy shop owner gives the firefighters a present—
a toy fire engine.
"Bye-bye." The firefighters wave.
Captain Kelly drives them back to the station.

Now Captain Kelly and the other very hungry firefighters sit down to eat their delicious spaghetti dinner. But suddenly—

DING! DING! DING! DING! The alarm rings.
They run to the fire truck.
WOOOOOOO!
Captain Kelly drives quickly.
Where's the fire?
"Help! Help!"
There—at the pet store!
Captain Kelly hooks up the hose to the hydrant.
Fire! Fire! Hotter! Hotter!
Hurry! Hurry! Water! Water!
The team works hard together.
Can they put out the fire?

Yes!
The pet store owner gives the firefighters a present—
a pet parrot.
"Bye-bye." The firefighters wave.
"Awwk! Bye-bye," says the parrot.
Captain Kelly drives them back to the station.

Now Captain Kelly and the other very, very hungry firefighters sit down to eat their delicious spaghetti dinner. But suddenly—

DING! DING! DING! DING! The alarm rings.
They run to the fire truck.
WOOOOOOO!
Captain Kelly drives quickly.
Where's the fire?
"Help! Help!"
There—at the bakery!
Captain Kelly hooks up the hose to the hydrant.
Fire! Fire! Hotter! Hotter!
Hurry! Hurry! Water! Water!
The team works hard together.
Can they put out the fire?

Bakery

Yes!
The baker gives the firefighters a present—
a fancy cake.
"Bye-bye." The firefighters wave.
Captain Kelly drives them back to the station.

Now Captain Kelly and the other very, very, very hungry firefighters sit down.

**Ssshhh . . . the alarm is quiet.
The firefighters eat their delicious spaghetti dinner
and their fancy cake. With ice cream!**

After dinner they try out the toy fire engine
and talk to the parrot.

Captain Kelly starts to yawn.
What a night! What a team!
The firefighters worked hard together to put out all the fires.
Captain Kelly is proud of everyone.
The firehouse is quiet.
Now there's only one more thing to put out.
Turn off the light, Captain Kelly.

Good night.

"AWWK! DING! DING! DING! AWWK!

WOOOOOOOOO! AWWK! BYE-BYE!"